Bright **Summaries**.com

Limonov

by Emmanuel Carrère

Limonov

BY EMMANUEL CARRÈRE

EMMANUEL CARRÈRE

Writer, screenwriter and director

- Born in 1957 in Paris
- Some of his works:
  - *The Snow Class* (1995), novel
  - *Other Lives Than Mine* (2009), novel
  - *Limonov* (2011), novel

Born in 1957 in Paris, Emmanuel Carrère is a writer, screenwriter and director. Son of historian and academic Hélène Carrère d'Encausse, a specialist in Russia, he started out as a film critic before turning to fiction in 1983 with his first novel, *L'Amie du jaguar*. Since then, he has been published by POL and won the Prix Fémina in 1995 for *La Classe de neige*. Since *L'Adversaire* (2000), which recounts the Jean-Claude Romand affair, Emmanuel Carrère has put fiction aside to devote himself to writing documentaries and stories, such as *Un roman russe* (2007) and *D'autres vies que la mienne* (2009). After collaborating on TV films as a scriptwriter, he turned to directing himself by adapting his novel *La Moustache* for the cinema in 2005.

LIMONOV

Limonov or the portrait of a gargantuan man

- **Genre:** autofiction

- **Reference edition:** *Limonov*, Paris, P.O.L., 2011, 496 p.

- **1st edition:** 2011

- **Themes:** investigation, violence, Russia, history

Limonov, published in 2011 and awarded the Prix Renaudot the same year, is the author's twelfth book. Continuing the Carrère family's interest in Russia, *Limonov* paints a portrait of a key figure in contemporary Russia, whom Carrère met on several occasions: Edward Limonov, a respected hero in Russia, a charismatic dissident and a neo-fascist thug. Halfway between investigation and fiction, history book and adventure novel, *Limonov* attempts to unravel the mystery of Carrère's fascination with this complex character, while tracing the history of Russia since the Second World War, the decline of communism and the fall of the Berlin Wall.

SUMMARY

THE INVESTIGATION INTO EDWARD LIMONOV

In 2006, Emmanuel Carrère was sent to Russia after the assassination of Anna Politkovskaya, a journalist and outspoken opponent of Vladimir Putin, then head of government. At the annual commemoration of the Dubrovka theatre massacre, he recognised Edward Limonov, whom he had met in Paris in the early 1980s.

👁 GOOD TO KNOW: DUBROVKA THEATRE MASSACRE

On 23 October 2002, about 50 Chechen rebels took 850 spectators hostage in the Dubrovka theatre in Moscow during a musical for young people. On 26 October, Russian forces violently put an end to the hostage-taking, killing 39 terrorists and at least 129 hostages.

Is Limonov "an ugly fascist, leading a militia of *skin-heads*" or "the hero of the democratic struggle in Russia" (p. 20)? Carrère decides to investigate. The objective: "To make these images coincide: the writer-voyou I once knew, the hunted guerrilla, the responsible politician, the star to whom the *celebrity* pages of magazines devote enamoured articles." (p. 30) He also wants to answer this question: is Limonov really a "bastard" (p. 35)?

FROM CHILDHOOD TO ADULTHOOD

Edward Savenko was born on 2 February 1943. His family moved to Kharkov (Ukraine) in 1947. He was a young ruffian whose discovery of literature (Romain Rolland, Jack London, Knut Hamsun) gave him the ambition to become a poet. Five years later, however, he was neither a thug nor a poet, but a foundryman. After a suicide attempt and an internment in an asylum, he became a salesman at the 41 bookshop, where all the decadent artists and poets of Kharkov met. He then started writing again and moved in with Anna Moiseyevna Rubinstein, the main saleswoman at 41, who had become his mistress. He invents a name for himself: Ed Limonov, in 'homage to his acidic and belligerent mood, for *limon* means lemon and *limonkagrenade* – that which pulls the pin' (p. 85). He then meets the painter Brusilovsky, who comes from Moscow and becomes his protector there.

In 1967, Limonov moved to Moscow, where he attended the poetry seminar of Arseni Tarkovsky (the father of Andrei, the film-maker) and made his debut as a poet in the Moscow underground. As for Anna, she was interned, then returned to Kharkov. Limonov married Elena, whom he had met at Brusilovsky's house. They were expelled from the country for dissidence, or more precisely for "convinced anti-Sovietism".

He then left for New York where he worked for a Russian daily newspaper while frequenting social events. At the beginning of 1976, Elena left him for a photographer.

The time of glitter is over: Edward lives in a shabby hotel, becomes a homosexual out of spite, reads Trotsky and starts writing again, not poetry, but the story of what he has just experienced, which will become *I, Editchka*. The novel was published in the autumn of 1980 under the title given to it by Jean-Jacques Pauvert, publisher of the Surrealists and the Marquis de Sade: *Le poète russe préfère les grands nègres.*

Limonov meets Jenny, the housekeeper of billionaire Steven Grey, and replaces her for a year in that position.

THE COMMITMENT

Emmanuel Carrère recalls his own youth and the fame of his mother, who was recognised as a specialist in the Soviet world. Fascinated by Limonov's life, in comparison with which his own seemed increasingly "dull and mediocre" (p. 221), Carrère interviewed the writer for the radio at the same time that *Diary of a Failure* was being published and Limonov became a "little star" (p. 230) in Paris.

Invited to New York in 1982 by his American publisher, Limonov brought with him Natacha Medvedeva, a singer, alcoholic and nymphomaniac, with whom he was to marry. At the same time, he met Jean-Édern Hallier, who had just relaunched *L'Idiot international*, a scandalous newspaper in which the extreme left and the extreme right rubbed shoulders. Limonov was then invited to Moscow where he discovered with disgust the free Russia, subjected to money and mafia. He goes in search of Natacha, who has disappeared in the city.

In 1991, Carrère reported from Yugoslavia. On his return, he wrote a biography of Philip K. Dick and followed, from afar, the emergence of the Serbo-Croat conflict. He also wrote about the August 1991 putsch in Russia, where the military tried to overthrow Boris Yeltsin, and the suspension of the activities of the Communist Party.

While invited to Belgrade for the publication of one of his books, Limonov is taken to the heart of the conflict by Serbian soldiers. He decides to support their cause, which makes him 'go from being a charming adventurer to a quasi-criminal of war among his Parisian friends' (p. 320).

Limonov met Alexander Dugin, a philosopher and fascist. Together they founded the National-Bolshevik Party and the newspaper *Limonka*. He then went from being a writer to a 'professional warrior and revolutionary' (p. 351). A few months later, Emmanuel Carrère met Zakhar Prilepine, a member of the National-Bolshevik Party.

After Yeltsin's victory in the elections, Limonov left for Belgrade and joined the Serbs as a soldier: he took part in several guerrilla actions.

When he returned to Moscow in 1994, he found himself a famous writer. His stay in the country was short-lived because, when Putin was elected head of Russia, he left for the Altaï mountains in Kazakhstan to follow a survival course. He was arrested by the special forces.

IMPRISONMENT

Limonov was then imprisoned in Lefortovo, 'where the most dangerous enemies of the state are put' (p. 434). He reads, writes and, after fifteen months of rigorous isolation, is transferred to Saratov, on the Volga, where his trial is to take place: he is accused of terrorism, organising or participating in an armed gang, acquiring, transporting, selling or stockpiling firearms, and inciting extremist activities.

Finally sentenced to four years' imprisonment, he was transferred to Engels, a labour camp where living conditions are very harsh. On 3 February 2003, he learned of the death of Natacha, his ex-wife, who had become an alternative rock figure.

Some time later, he was released early under the television cameras. In this way, Limonov '[became] the star in his country that he dreamed of being: an adored writer, a worldly guerrilla, a good client for the *celebrity* press' (p. 475).

After four years of investigation, Emmanuel Carrère admits that he has not been able to remove the ambiguity of the character. Limonov thus remains an extremely complex man, capable of taking on many different roles.

CHARACTER STUDY

LIMONOV

Brilliant and non-conformist, he is 'a living legend' (p. 32). But beyond that, it is difficult to describe him: he is an eminently complex, multifaceted character. A poet and a politician, a soldier and a valet, a man of power and a tramp, a fascist and a democrat, his life, like his own, runs the gamut – from poverty to fame, from politics to the art world, from the factory to prison. She makes him the hero of a modern, violent and fascinating adventure novel.

This heroic – and at the same time romantic, sulphurous, daring and talented – life is the one Limonov dreamed of as a child: as a boy he 'doesn't want to be like his father when he grows up. He doesn't want an honest and slightly stupid life, but a free and dangerous one: a man's life' (p. 53). It will be the life of a thug, but never the life of 'a second-knife' (p. 63): that of 'a king of crime' (p. 63). This very romantic vision of existence, ignoring material contingencies, and constantly asserting righteousness and inner nobility, makes Limonov a magnificent incarnation of the hero. On the other hand, it is undoubtedly this ability not to betray his dreams that makes the character so charismatic, far from the half-measures and lukewarmness of ordinary, more comfortable lives.

His quest for public recognition, his vocation as a gang leader and his passion for pretty women give him an almost childish and endearing character. How then can he be this unsympathetic guy, at once contemptuous of the weak and envious of the powerful, fascinated by brute force, obsessed with virility? Carrère finally finds this definition: Limonov is 'a magnificent being, capable of monstrous acts' (p. 386).

CARRÈRE

The self-portrait that Carrère timidly sketches forms the absolute counterpoint to the figure of Limonov:

- They have different social backgrounds (Carrère portrays himself as a young bourgeois with a fledgling literary career, overwhelmed by the Parisian success of Limonov in the early 1980s);

- They follow different trajectories (Carrère's is a straightforward, linear, predictable one, whereas Limonov's follows improbable upheavals);

- They develop different political sensibilities (Carrère the democrat cannot but be deeply disturbed by Limonov's neo-fascist leanings, especially as they are fully assumed).

Yet there are parallels: beyond anecdotal points, what brings Limonov and Carrère together is mainly an ability to read the world and to order it according to the principle of the strongest.

- Limonov submits totally to this fascist reading grid: it conditions his vision of the world and confirms him in his quest for power. Fascinated by virility, by male fraternity, he dreams of escaping the modest, even mediocre, life promised to him by his origins; he is 'plagued by the anguish of being part of the second category' (p. 221). His trajectory must therefore be anything but banal: what he does (poetry or politics), he does with excess, panache and singularity.

- Carrère explicitly places himself on the side of the defeated, incapable of the flamboyance of his subject: his strange insistence on comparing himself to Limonov throughout the text nevertheless reflects the same tendency to classify men – the powerful and the others – and above all the same fascination for the powerful. And the reader is simultaneously forced into a hierarchy. But for Carrère, as for us, is it not a question of freeing ourselves from this natural tendency to hierarchise, as this Buddhist quotation testifies: "The man who judges himself superior, inferior or even equal to another man does not understand reality" (p. 227)? To leave this dualistic vision of the world would thus mean, according to Carrère, to attain wisdom.

READING KEYS

THE HISTORY OF RUSSIA

Violence is the common thread in Carrère's long portrait of Russia. On the immense field of ruins that is the country at the end of the Second World War (twenty-six million Soviets died in the war, as many are homeless) only poverty, illiteracy and alcoholism flourish. But to understand Russia at that time, it is important to go back further in the country's history.

From the Russian Revolution of 1917 to the death of Stalin in 1953

With the Russian Revolution of 1917, the Bolsheviks overthrew the Tsarist regime and imposed the dictatorship of the proletariat with the slogan "Factories to the workers, land to the peasants, peace to the people!" After Lenin's death in 1924, the advent of Joseph Stalin at the head of the Communist Party, between 1927 and 1929, marked the launch of a brutal and radical transformation of Soviet society. In a few years, the face of the USSR was profoundly changed by agricultural collectivisation and industrialisation. However, the economic modernisation of the country required enormous labour demands, whether imposed or agreed, and the transformation of society was accompanied by a policy of massive repression. With millions of victims, but carefully concealed by the regime, in a context of total indoctrination, this policy opened a long period of terror and denunciation, marked in particular by the great purges and the considerable expansion of forced labour camps (gulag).

Nikita Khrushchev's regime (1953-1964)

Until 1953, the date of Stalin's death – which paradoxically plunged the country into despair – Stalinist repression was in full swing. With Nikita Khrushchev, First Secretary of the Communist Party of the Soviet Union from March 1953 to October 1964, the regime became more flexible. In 1956, the eponymous report read out at the XX Party Congress denounced the cult of personality under Stalin and acknowledged Stalinist repression. Khrushchev presented himself as the main inspirer of the policy of de-Stalinisation at home and of peaceful coexistence abroad.

With the authorisation of the publication of Solzhenitsyn's first title (a Russian writer and dissident who opposed Soviet oppression), *A Day of Ivan Denissovich*, in 1962, the USSR was shocked: "No [book], except for *The Gulag Archipelago*, ten years later, has so *truly* changed the course of history." (p. 89) This is the time of the thaw and the denunciation of the camps, where twenty million Russians are said to have died during the twenty-five years of Stalin's reign. *The Gulag Archipelago was published* in France and the United States in 1974 and states that "the Gulag [...] is not a disease of the Soviet system but its essence and even its purpose" (p. 129).

From 1964 to the collapse of the Soviet bloc

From Leonid Brezhnev to Mikhail Gorbachev, via Yuri Andropov and Konstantin Chernenko, Carrère evokes the successive governments of the USSR from 1964 to 1991, from a narrow conservatism to a desire for *glasnost* (transparency). Finally, Gorbachev (in power from 1985 to 1991), a resolute reformer, launched the economic, cultural and political liberalisation of the USSR – called *perestroika*. In this way, he made history freely available and brought about the collapse and decay of the Soviet bloc.

It was with the coming to power of Boris Yeltsin, the first president of the new Russian Federation (from 1991 to 1999), that the Russian economy really entered its phase of liberalisation, 'without rules of the game, without laws, without a banking system, without taxation' (p. 336): 'For a million fools who [...] began to get rich frantically, a hundred and fifty million people plunged into misery.' (p. 338) His actions are generally considered negative by a large part of the Russian population: the massive privatisations, the attempt to make a brutal transition to a market economy, the corruption in the highest spheres of power, as well as the media wars between political and economic competitors explain, among other things, the indifference and disapproval that the Russian population feels towards him.

Carrère finally evokes the emergence of the Chechen conflict in 1994, then the arrival in power of Vladimir Putin in 2000 who leads the country with an iron fist, crushing all democratic opposition.

FASCISM AND THE CONFUSION OF IDEOLOGIES

How can one be the founder of a fascist party, the National-Bolshevik Party, and ally oneself with the democrats of the other Russia, to the point of being recognised as one of the last major opponents of Vladimir Putin? How can one call for the return of Stalin while claiming to be a democrat? Radically opposed positions taken by the same man, Limonov. How can this be explained?

In reality, nothing has filled the void left by the fall of the Wall and the disintegration of the Soviet system; nothing has come to make sense of the disqualification of communist ideology, especially not the dictatorship of the market, its injustice, its cynicism. Out of this rises a deep disarray and an obvious nostalgia for a time when things made sense and people were proud of themselves and their country. Fascism responds to this disarray because it rejects the uncertainties and questioning inherent in democratic progress: above all, fascism gives simple and definitive answers that make it easier to grasp reality and reduce its complexity.

But more than a real fascist, Limonov is first and foremost an opponent of any system, and his *nazbols* are above all people left behind, rebels, often members of the Russian counterculture. More than a real fascist, Limonov is a huge punk, playing with provocations and aggressiveness, praising vital energy, strength and virility. His capacity for self-doubt and his integrity make him a childlike and heroic character: in a word, fascinating.

THE RUSSIAN LITERARY SCENE

After a relative freedom of creation between 1918 and 1929 – years marked by Futurism or Expressionism – the Russian artistic milieu was strongly repressed under the Stalinist government, which tried to impose with violence the style of Soviet realism, which consisted of a questionable alliance between art, ideology and politics. Official art then became a support for the government's policy, a real propaganda tool. Art would either be proletarian or it would not: all other trends were seen as resurgences of bourgeois art and therefore severely repressed. Censored, many writers were imprisoned and killed or starved to death, like Ossip Mandelstam, Isaac Babel and Boris Pilniak. Andrei Platonov worked as a caretaker and was not allowed to publish.

Carrère describes the Russian literary milieu with finesse, deciphering its contradictions and subtleties. Thus, it appears that perhaps never before has the separation between official literature, under the thumb of the politicians, and *underground* culture, free and authentic, truly challenging, been so marked as in the Soviet system. The functioning of the paranoid and crushing bureaucratic system has generated a confusion between the literary and the political spheres, as we have just seen in the previous paragraph: through censorship, the system has endorsed authors and works that fit into the very rigid framework of Soviet realism; through censorship, an author is official – "success [...] clearly designates [a poet] as a sell-out and an impostor" (p. 79) – or is not – "the advantage of censorship is that you can be an author who does not publish anything without being suspected of lacking talent, on the contrary." (p. 79) The myth of the cursed author then has its heyday: "The genius must be not only unrecognized but drunk, delirious, socially maladjusted" (p. 80), a stay in a psychiatric hospital being worth "a patent for *dissidence*" (p. 80). Any artist who is settled, recognised and living in comfort is then suspected of dishonesty, whereas 'an authentic artist [is] necessarily a failure' (p. 113).

THE GENDER ISSUE

The title of the book, this sober *Limonov*, anchors the work a priori in the territory of biography. Whether it is hagiographic or critical is not the problem (in fact, it is both simultaneously), but the affirmation of the genre is disturbed by the author's incessant digressions.

Carrère interferes with the text on several levels:

- He is first of all the honest man who questions Limonov's ambiguity, his complexity and his undeniable charm. This fascination for Limonov is disturbing, in the strongest sense of the term. It disturbs Carrère, who does not understand how this figure who embodies values so far removed from his own can prove so attractive; it upsets his certainties and forces him to question his prejudices. This fascination simultaneously disturbs the reader, who is also forced to free himself from all his automatisms;

- By the autobiographical indications with which he scatters the text, he is also the inverted mirror of Limonov's figure, the figure of the average man whom everything opposes to the hero. This unexpected presence disrupts the traditional linearity of the biography and contradicts the biographer's supposed dedication to his subject - all the more so since Carrère is also a character in the story;

- Finally, he is present as an author confronted with the difficulties that successively presented themselves to him during the writing process - difficulties that he shares with us, citing his career as a journalist, his documentary and literary sources, and his embarrassment in evoking certain episodes in Limonov's life.

This presence of the author in a work dedicated to another is a recurring element in Carrère's writing since *L'Adversaire*: the subject of each book is not so much the announced biography of such and such a character, but rather the interaction that takes place between the character and the author.

The blurring of the lines between fiction and reality will also be examined: since *L'Adversaire*, in fact, this has been a major constant in Carrère's writing. The documentary nature of *Limonov* is indisputable (four years of investigation), but this raw material is filtered through the author's subjectivity, which reconstructs reality.

FOOD FOR THOUGHT

A FEW QUESTIONS TO DEEPEN YOUR REFLECTION...

- Emmanuel Carrère places this quote from Vladimir Putin at the beginning of the book: "He who wants to restore communism has no head. He who does not regret it has no heart." With regard to contemporary Russian history, comment.

- Like all of Emmanuel Carrère's books since *The Adversary*, everything is real, nothing is invented. Yet Carrère presents his *Limonov* as the most romantic book of his career. Explain.

- How does the biographer interfere with the autobiography?

- The fascination (a mixture of attraction and repulsion) for Limonov is accompanied by a flagrant masochism in the autobiographical indications. What do you think Carrère's project is?

- How can extremes in politics come together, despite radically opposed positions?

- Is a hero necessarily a positive figure?

- Is a bourgeois necessarily a negative figure?

TO GO FURTHER

REFERENCE EDITION

CARRÈRE E., *Limonov*, Paris, P.O.L Éditeur, 2011.

Emmanuel Carrère received the 2011 French Language Prize for *Limonov*. He was not considered for the Goncourt but won the Renaudot Prize.

SOME OF LIMONOV'S WORKS

Mes prisons, translated from Russian by Antonina Roubichoi-Stretz, Paris, Actes Sud, 2009.

Journal d'un raté, translated from Russian by Antoine Pingaud, Paris, Albin Michel, 2011.

Discours d'une grande gueule coiffée d'une casquette de prolo, preceded by *Salade niçoise and Écrivain international*, Paris, Le Dilettante, 2011.

La Grande Époque, Paris, Flammarion, «Fiction étrange» collection, 1992.

Le poète russe préfère les grands nègres, Paris, Pauvert/Ramsay, 1979.

Le Dos de Mme Chatain, Paris, Le Dilettante, 1993.

Your opinion is important to us!
Leave a comment on the website of your online bookshop
and share your favourites on social networks!

Bright ≡Summaries.com

More guides to rediscover your love of literature

The Catcher in the Rye
BY J. D. SALINGER

Harry Potter and the Chamber of Secrets
BY J.K. ROWLING

I Know Why the Caged Bird Sings
BY MAYA ANGELOU

Normal People
BY SALLY ROONEY

Eleanor Oliphant is Completely Fine
BY GAIL HONEYMAN

One Hundred Years of Solitude
BY GABRIEL GARCÍA MÁRQUEZ

www.BrightSummaries.com

Ebook EAN: 9782808686730
Paperback EAN: 9782808698139
Legal Deposit: D/2023/12603/1093

Cover: © Primento
Digital conception by Primento, the digital partner of publishers.